My "s" Sound Box®

WRITTEN BY JANE BELK MONCURE • ILLUSTRATED BY REBECCA THORNBURGH

The Child's World®
childsworld.com

Published by The Child's World®
1980 Lookout Drive • Mankato, MN 56003-1705
800-599-READ • www.childsworld.com

ISBN HARDCOVER: 9781503823228
ISBN PAPERBACK: 9781503831445
LCCN: 2017960384

Printed in the United States of America
PA02371

A NOTE TO PARENTS AND EDUCATORS:

Magic moon machines and five fat frogs are just a few of the fun things you can share with children by reading books with them. Reading aloud helps children in so many ways! It introduces them to new words, motivates them to develop their own reading skills, and expands their attention span and listening abilities. So it's important to find time each day to share a book or two . . . or three!

As you read with young children, you can help develop their understanding of how print works by talking about the parts of the book—the cover, the title, the illustrations, and the words that tell the story. As you read, use your finger to point to each word, modeling a gentle sweep from left to right.

Simple word games help develop important prereading skills, including an understanding of rhyme and alliteration (when words share the same beginning sound, such as "six" and "sand"). Try playing with words from a book you've just shared: "What other words start with the same sound as moon?" "Cat and hat, do those words rhyme?" The possibilities are endless—and so are the rewards!

My "s" Sound Box®

Little had a box. "I will find things that begin with my **S** sound," he said.

"I will put them into my sound box."

Little took off his shoes, socks, sweater, and shirt. Did he put his shoes, socks, sweater, and shirt into his box? He did.

Little put on his swimsuit and his sandals.

He went for a walk on the sand.

He found a shovel and a sand pail. He made

a sand castle. Then he put the shovel, the

sand pail, and the sand castle into his box.

Little  went for a swim in the sea.

He saw a seal swimming in the sea.

He saw six more seals on the sand. Did he

put the seven seals into his box? He did.

Little found seashells all over the sand.

He also found a starfish. Did he put the seashells

and the starfish into his box? He did.

Then he saw a shark. It was a small

shark. So Little slipped it into a sack.

He put the sack into the box.

Then Little saw a sea snake. It was a small sea snake. So he slipped the snake into the sack. He put the sack back into the box.

Later, Little met a sailor.

The sailor gave him a sailor hat.

"Let's play!" said the sailor.

They played on the seesaw.

They slid down the slide.

They swung on the swings.

Suddenly, there was a big noisy sound!

The sound was coming from the box.

"What is in the box?"

asked the sailor.

"Things that begin with my **S** sound," said Little .

"I sail on things that begin with your **S** sound," said the sailor. "I sail on a ship."

"And I sail on a submarine."

The sailor helped Little bring his box into the submarine. Little took his things out of his box.

Little and the sailor drew pictures of the ship, the swing, the slide, and the seesaw.

Little 's Word List

sack

sailor

sailor hat

sand

sandal

sand castle

sand pail

sea

seal

seashell

sea snake

seesaw

shark

ship

shirt

shoe

shovel

slide

sock

starfish

submarine

sweater

swimsuit

swing

Other Words with Little

salad	snow	squirrel
sandwich	soap	stamp
saw	soup	star
seed	spider	stick
skunk	spoon	stop sign
snail	square	sun

More to Do!

Little and the sailor talked about lots of different **S** words. They put many **S** things into the box. You can make **S** cards of all the things.

What you need:

- index cards
- crayons
- markers
- yarn
- hole punch tool

Directions:

1. Draw a picture of these words on the index cards:

- sack
- sand pail
- seal
- sea snake

- shark
- ship
- shoe
- sock

- starfish
- swing

2. After you have your picture cards, have an adult help you sort the pictures into two piles: sea creatures and not-sea creatures.

3. Put all the cards together again. Now sort the cards into two new piles: things you play with and things you don't play with.

4. Put all the cards together again. Now try writing each word below the picture you drew. Have an adult help you write down the sounds you hear in each word.

5. Now use the hole-punching tool to make a hole in the corner of each card. Pull some yarn through and make your very own "s" book!

About the Author

Best-selling author Jane Belk Moncure (1926–2013) wrote more than 300 books throughout her teaching and writing career. After earning a master's degree in early childhood education from Columbia University, she became one of the pioneers in that field. In 1956, she helped form the Virginia Association for Early Childhood Education, which established the first statewide standards for teachers of young children.

Inspired by her work in the classroom, Mrs. Moncure's books became standards in primary education, and her name was recognized across the country. Her success was reflected not only in her books' popularity with parents, children, and educators, but also by numerous awards, including the 1984 C. S. Lewis Gold Medal Award.

About the Illustrator

Rebecca Thornburgh lives in a pleasantly spooky old house in Philadelphia. If she's not at her drawing table, she's reading—or singing with her band, called Reckless Amateurs. Rebecca has one husband, two daughters, and two silly dogs.